THE DOG

RULES

THE DOG RULES

by Coco La Rue
illustrated by Kyla May

Scholastic Inc.
New York Toronto London Auckland
Sydney Mexico City New Delhi Hong Kong

ISBN 978-0-545-28261-1

12 11 10 9 8 7 6 5 4   11 12 13 14 15 16/0

Printed in the U.S.A.   40
First printing, January 2011

Book design by Jennifer Rinaldi Windau

To Cow, Cleveland,
Hazel, and Horace—
great cats,* one and all
— C.L.R.

To Jaida, Kiara & Mikka
(my three gorgeous girls),
Luv U heaps, ♥ Mummy xxx
— K.M.

* Of course, they'd be even greater if they were birds, but
  I'll let that slide for these champs.

TABLE OF CONTENTS

* It is vital that you read this memo. Failure to do so will result in the evaporation and/or explosion of this book. Well, not really. But read it anyway. As a favor to me. Pretty please?!?

MEMO

TO: Readers of this book*
SUBJECT: Classified information

This is a very important questionnaire to determine your eligibility to read the following pages.

1. Are you human?
      A) Yes!
      B) Woof?
      C) What did you call me, you imp?

2. Do you know how to read?
      A) Yes!
      B)
      C) Why, I invented the English language, you scoundrel!

3. Are you a cat person or a dog person?
      A) Yes!
      B) Dogs rule!
      C) That's personal, thank you very much.

4. Do you follow or flout the rules?
      A) Yes!
      B) Is flout a type of dessert?
      C) How dare you insult me, you scalawag!

If you answered mostly:

      A's) Fantabulous! Read this book. Then ask your teacher to read it to your class. Then petition the government to make it a law that everyone in the U.S.A. read this book every single day.

      B's) Arf! Take a flea bath. Then read this book.

      C's) Why so angry? This book might make you angrier. Read it at your own risk. You've been warned.

* That's you.

meet THE Lanes

Darling reader, my name is Coco La Rue. In these pages you will hear about a monstrous mutt called **Monty**. Even the mention of that miserable name makes me shudder.

Monty is owned by a decent breed of humans who have only one flaw—they let that mutt get away with everything. My goal here is simple: to have the big hairy human banish **Monty** forever so I can live in peace as a bird of my breeding should.

Who are the Lanes? Let me introduce you to them. . . .

This is the hairy human. The short one calls him "Dad." The pretty one calls him "Sweet Buns." The Pima Panthers call him **"COACH."**

NAME:
**COACH
WALKER
LANE**

SIZE: **BIG. REALLY BIG. BIG ENOUGH TO BANISH THE BEAST!**

FAVORITE PLAYS: **THE BLITZ AND THE QUARTERBACK SACK**

PET PEEVE: **RUNNING OUT OF MEAT LOAF**

MEMBER OF: **SNEAKER OF THE WEEK CLUB**

Ah, Aurora, the pretty human. She sings all day long. We are birds of a feather!

NAME:
Dr. Aurora Lane

HAIR COLOR: scarlet red, like the beautiful cardinal

FAVORITE PIZZA TOPPINGS: arugula and artichokes

TALENT: total recall for action movies

MEMBER OF: Meditation for the Masses

The small human. He is too friendly with that pampered pooch.

NAME:
Parker Lane

DREAM BIRTHDAY GIFT: stormtrooper helmet and lightsaber

ACTUAL BIRTHDAY GIFT: handmade sweater from Grandpa

STRANGEST PHYSICAL FEATURE: freckles in the shape of the Big Dipper

WORST QUALITY: loves Monty

I've already introduced myself. But let me add that I am exceedingly talented and refined. Unlike some animals I know.

NAME:

Coco La Rue

PET PEEVE: messes, mutts, and misbehaving

HOBBIES: flight, song, and Sudoku

FAVORITE FOOD: mango salsa

MEMBER OF: The Official Order of the Big-Brained Birds

Monty is an odious creature. He is dull, dim-witted, and dirty. And, frankly, he smells.

NAME:
Monty Lane

BIRTHDAY: **April Fool's Day**

FAVORITE PLACE TO BE SCRATCHED: **starts with a B, ends with an UTT.**

FUR COLOR: **mustard yellow, pencil-shaving gray, or blueberry***

MEMBER OF: **The Slobber Society**

*It depends on what's in the trash can.

THE NAME GAME

Parker thought long and hard about the perfect name for Monty. But what if Monty had been named something different?

MAJOR

Milton Jefferson Harrison III

JUSTIN TIMBERPOOCH

chadwick

BOND.
Fido Bond.

Sweet reader, look at this awful photo of the Almost-Perfect Lane Family.

Now place your thumb, or two pennies, or a gherkin pickle over that hideous creature. And look at the result: a charming picture!

I.
Will.
Get.
This.
Mutt.
Banished.

Just you wait and see.

My request to you, dearest reader, is this: Hear my tale, and if you are like-minded, simply sign the petition at the back of this book, get 1,400 of your friends to do the same, and send the entire mess of signatures to my:

Banish the Mutt!
Campaign

care of the Almost-Perfect Lane Family.*

* Okay, so there isn't a petition in this book. But you could start one, couldn't you? For me? Pretty please?

CHOOSING A NAME FOR YOUR PET

Please note: A name that is sweet when uttered in the privacy of your own home may sound sour when hollered in a dark alley.*

Whatever you do, DON'T name your pet:

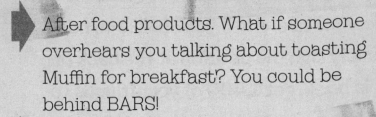 After food products. What if someone overhears you talking about toasting Muffin for breakfast? You could be behind BARS!

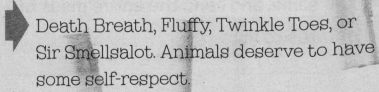 Death Breath, Fluffy, Twinkle Toes, or Sir Smellsalot. Animals deserve to have some self-respect.

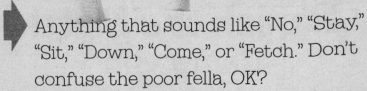 Anything that sounds like "No," "Stay," "Sit," "Down," "Come," or "Fetch." Don't confuse the poor fella, OK?

* The author of this book does not recommend going into dark alleys unless you are accompanied by a kindergarten production of *I Once Was a Little Bumblebee*. With all those six-year-olds running around, nothing bad can happen.

Chapter 2

RULES RULE

My Campaign of Complete and Utter Dog Banishment is progressing nicely, thanks to the carelessness of the crude canine. He simply *cannot* behave!

"Oh, Monty! I'll **never** find my wedding ring if you distract me with those **stink bombs!**"

"Fuss with my sanctuary all you like, you ignorant ingrate. You'll pay dearly."

"HEY! WHAT THE—? PAWS OFF MY MEAT-LOAF OMELET!"

And when Monty can't behave, the hairy one goes ballistic.

Listen to Coach rant! He is at the end of his rope!

Beloved reader, I've learned a lot about humans during my time in the Almost-Perfect Lane household.

For instance: Big, hairy humans love rules. And humans with whistles around their neck love numbers. Therefore, **big, hairy, whistle-wearing humans love numbered rules!**

Coach has a rule for just about everything.

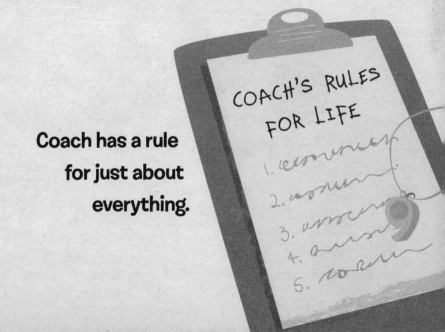

COACH'S RULES FOR LIFE

1.
2.
3.
4.
5.

COACH'S RULES FOR LIFE*

1. DRESS TO IMPRESS!

Coach says, "Are you wearing breathable fabric? Is there a respected sports team on your shirt? Are your socks pulled to the top of your calf? Check! Check! Check!"

* This is just a small glimpse inside the twisted mind of the man who holds Monty's future in the palm of his meaty hands.

2. GET THE JOB DONE!

Coach says, "Don't quit on your team! Don't quit on yourself! And definitely don't quit on deodorant!"

3. FAMILY TOGETHERNESS IS ESSENTIAL!

Coach says, "Lane Family Unit! Pedal on *one*. Love each other on *two*. *One, two! One, two!*"

Yes, Coach loves rules. He loves them the way . . .

. . . *bees love honey.*

. . . peanut butter loves jelly.

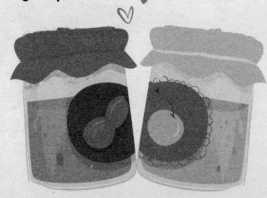

...fleas love dogs.

...DRYERS LOVE SOCKS.

The hairy one has rules just for Monty.

Rule #1: DON'T ACT LIKE A DOG.

Rule #2: GYM SHORTS ARE FOR WEARING, NOT FOR EATING.

Rule #3: DON'T EAT COACH'S MEAT LOAF.

Rule #4: THE COUCH IS A DOG-FREE ZONE.

Rule #5: IF YOUR NAME IS NOT "TRASH," STAY OUT OF THE CAN.

Rule #6: MR. FAMOUS* IS NOT A TOY.

Parker's precious pinhead couldn't abide by these rules if his life depended on it—**which it does!**

* You'll meet him later.

WE *WILL* FIND YOUR WEDDING RING, DEAR. FAN OUT!

Excellent idea, Sweet Buns. Parker, could you turn off the oven in 20 minutes and take out my meat loaf?

Mo-ooom! Don't call him Sweet Buns!

Now it's time to put my plan into action!

WHEN GOOD RULES GO UN-FOLLOWED,
OR THE WRATH OF COACH

DELINQUENT: Pima Panthers
OFFENSE: Showing up late to practice
PUNISHMENT: Wind sprints in full uniform

DELINQUENT: Lane Family Unit
OFFENSE: Arguing at the dinner table
PUNISHMENT: Extra L.F.U. togetherness

DELINQUENT: Monty
OFFENSE: Just about everything*
PUNISHMENT: If my plan works:
BANISHMENT!

* Including going berserk when it's time for walkies, a total lack of
table manners, and an unhealthy obsession with athletic attire..

Chapter 3

RULE #1

DON'T ACT LIKE A DOG

Monty, please behave!

If you don't, they'll send you to dog jail!

As **if!**

Lock the mutt up!

Or doggy boot camp!

Or ship you to the MOON!

Maybe the army can keep this dog in line.

Where **aliens** belong.

The short human is such a sweet boy! But he should not waste his time trying to get this tail-wagger to behave.

It's impossible!

Get Monty to behave? **Ha!** The small human would have an easier time teaching the sun not to set. **That fleabag cannot be trained!** The whole family has tried, but it's no use.

They don't leave snacks unattended.

They never need an alarm clock.

They can't even walk barefoot in the backyard.

They can't even call Coach by his first name. Because when they do . . .

...Monty thinks it's time for a WALK and
bolts out the door...

. . . to visit the cute Pomeranian down the block.

Since Monty can never think of anywhere else to go, one of the humans always finds him and drags him back home.

Too bad.

Watch this! Getting Monty to break even ONE of Coach's rules will be easy.

There he goes again. Breaking rules is all that mutt is cut out to do.

Soon the Lanes will need a new pet.
When selecting an animal companion,
one should always consider the unbiased
advice of my great-aunt Mimi:
DON'T GET A DOG!
Why, you ask?

1. Parrots have better
conversations.

2. Parrots are
more graceful.

3. Parrots know better tricks.

However, if **only** a dog will do,
look for these qualities:

curved ~~beak~~
snout

← elegant crest

seed eater →

tail that
molts in
the spring

FINDING THE PERFECT PET

For well-mannered humans, a parrot is the perfect pet.
But maybe you are a human of another sort. Take this quiz
to find out which pet is best for you.

1. You like your furniture:
    A) clean and neat, like the day it was purchased.
    B) drenched in slobber and drool.
    C) covered in scratches.

2. You like your pets to:
    A) engage you in lively conversation.
    B) chew up your favorite pair of slippers.
    C) ignore you.

3. You like pet food that smells like:
    A) fresh fruit and healthy nuts.
    B) the neighbor's trash.
    C) week-old fish.

If you answered mostly:

A's) Just as I suspected: You are smart and beautiful and
    kind. Buy a parrot and finally know what it is like to live a
    wonderful and meaningful life!

B's) Haven't you been paying attention? Dogs are horrible
    creatures!

C's) We have a serious problem on our hands. You should retake
    this quiz—it says you like cats!

Chapter 4

RULE #2

GYM SHORTS ARE FOR WEARING, NOT FOR EATING

Getting Monty to break Rule #2 shouldn't be hard. When most creatures see an old stinky sock, they see . . . an old stinky sock.

But not this mutt. Show Monty a stinky sock and he sees a big slice of **cheddar cheese.**

A closet full of silk dresses and wool sweaters looks like an **all-you-can-eat buffet** to this nincompoop.

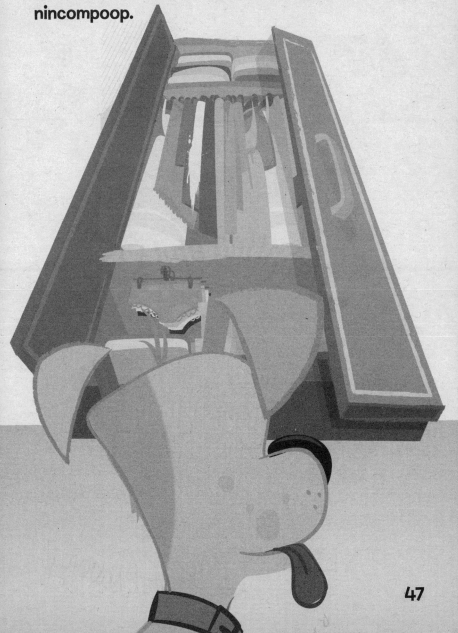

In Monty's twisted mind, shirts and shorts make excellent dog snacks.

Tempting and tasty!

Scrumptious and savory!

Syrupy and sweet!

=

Delicious and delectable!

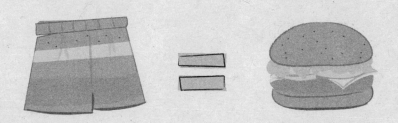

=

No item of clothing is safe from this dog.

Look at them!

The Almost-Perfect Lane Family has been ripped to shreds. Nothing can stop that carnivorous canine.

Monty eats the **seats** out of **jeans,** the **lace** off **dresses,** and the **heels** out of **socks.**

But even worse than the holes is the drool.

Icky,
sticky,
strands

Sewer-
scented
dribbles

Radioactive
blobs

Alas, the Lanes have tried **everything** to keep Monty from eating their clothes.

But never fear, Monty. Your dear aunt Coco is here to help.* I happen to have a spare key to the padlock.

On the menu today, a delicious meal of . . .

* Help get you banished forever, that is.

Stinky,
SMeLLy,
Gym SHORts.

Bon appétit!*

* French for "enjoy your meal." Enjoy it while you can,
Monty. It may be your last!

There is only **one thing** Monty likes to eat more, than gym shorts. . . .

Chapter 5

RULE #3

DON'T EAT COACH'S MEAT LOAF

Remember how much Coach loves rules? Double that, square it, then add your age and that's only half as much as Coach loves the loaf made of meat.

He has a library on the history of meat loaf...

... which helped him win 1st place in three meat-loaf eating competitions...

...which he celebrated
with a trip to the Meat Loaf
Museum of Art...

...which inspired
him to invent Musk of
Meat Loaf cologne.*

* Carried exclusively at Uncle Marty's House of Meat.

DING!

Let's make a deal, Monty. If you don't eat my dad's favorite thing in the entire world, I'll give you a ten-minute belly rub.

Did you hear that? Well, Parker's very tempting bribe won't be enough to keep Coach's precious loaf safe. Monty's already broken the first two rules. And as Coach says,

"THREE STRIKES AND YOU'RE OUT."

Next stop:

DOGGY JAIL!

And I think I can be of assistance again . . . I will distract Parker so Monty can get that meat!

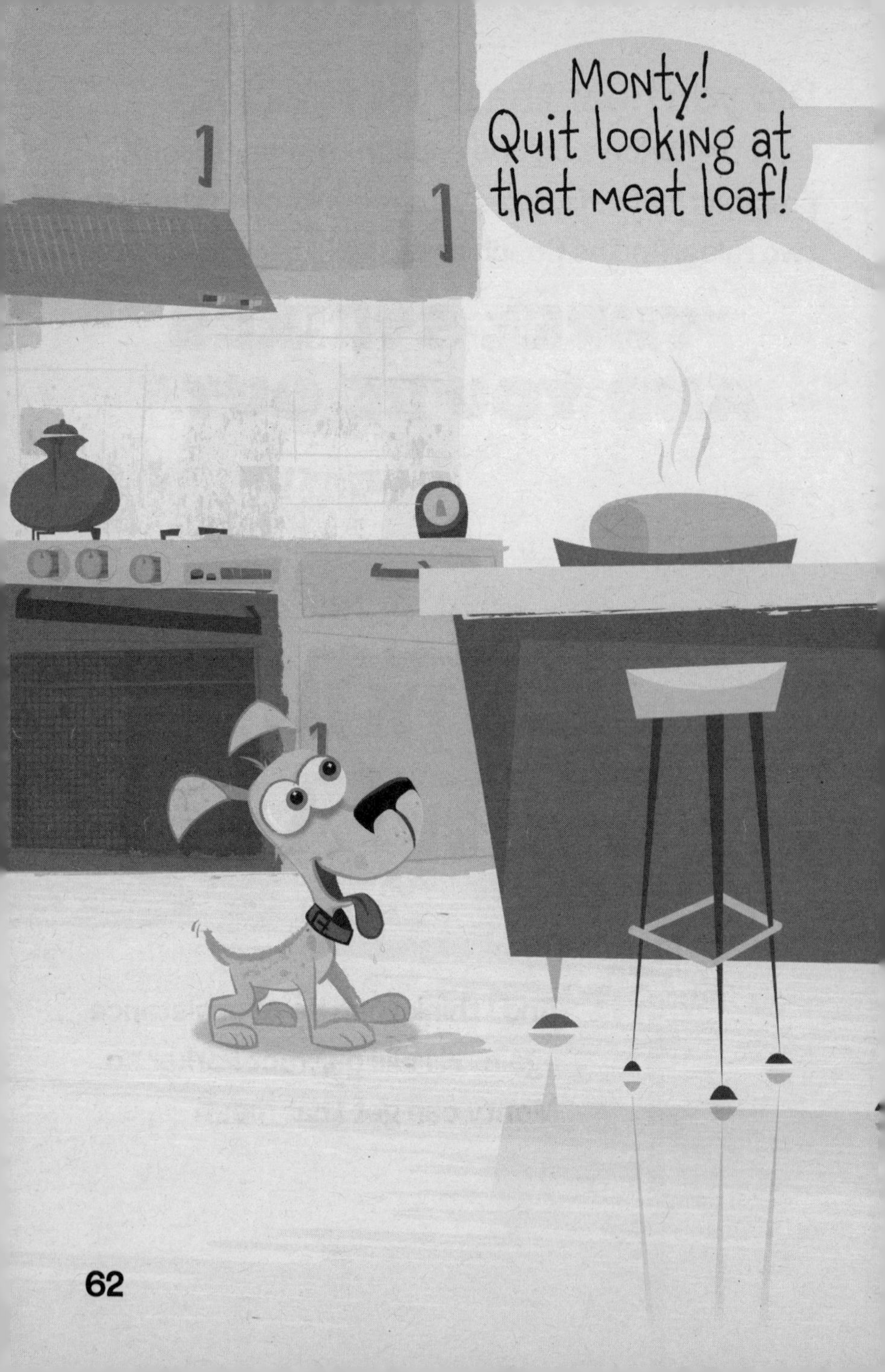
Monty!
Quit looking at
that meat loaf!

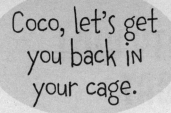

63

THINGS MONTY WILL NEVER EAT

Ice
Brain freeze makes him cranky.

Paint
He can't figure out how to get the lids off.

Dog food
Too easy. He needs the thrill of the hunt.

THINGS MONTY WOULD LOVE TO EAT

His weight in bacon
Some soggy, some crispy, please!

A gym-short smoothie
With just a hint of sweat sock for flavor.

A certain unsuspecting parrot
Comes with her own unique seasoning.

THINGS MONTY HAS ACTUALLY EATEN

78 cents

The pennies gave him indigestion.

A not-fast-enough lizard

Tickly!

A beautiful platter of just-baked, savory, scrumptious, mouth-watering meat loaf!

67

DO YOU SMELL THAT? MY LOAF SENSES ARE TINGLING. THE SWEET AROMA OF MY MEAT LOAF IS NOW TINGED WITH THE SMELL OF ... SLOBBER?!?

Arf!

Hee hee hee!
Ho ho ho!

My birthday is months away, but I think I'll be getting a present any moment now. My plan worked like a charm! I should write a book.* I'll call it *How to Banish a Brainless Mutt in Three Simple Steps.*

Mom! I found it!

Hmmm. Parker's voice sounds awfully happy for a boy about to lose his mutt.

Why isn't he sobbing uncontrollably?

* Parrots everywhere would be grateful.

Aurora's missing ring!

That clueless canine found it buried in the loaf! Now the humans will think that good-for-nothing is good for something!

'Atta boy, Monty!

My ring! It must have come off while I was making dinner!!

DOG! YOU DID GOOD. BUT THE NEXT TIME YOU TOUCH MY MEAT LOAF, YOU'RE OUTTA HERE!

Oh, dismal day!

To come so close to ridding
this house of that pesky pup,
and fail miserably.

How can I go on?

Buck up, old gal. He may have
won this battle, but you will
win the war.

Chapter 6

THE COUCH IS A DOG-FREE ZONE

Devoted reader, we've suffered a terrible setback.
But fear not! I am full of inspiration and flair,
while Monty is only full of ground beef. Which
makes him sleepy.

Very sleepy.

And when this crude creature is sleepy he heads
straight for . . .

74

... the couch!

Monty's been banned from the couch for life. But he can't help turning Coach's cave of comfort into a den of disorder. Pillows get tossed. Blankets get thrown. All while he settles in for a nice long nap.

I predict Monty will soon be taken away in pawcuffs!

Kind reader, see what indignities I am made to suffer? His sawing snores interrupt my scheming.

And the humans do **nothing!**
Perhaps his drool makes them powerless.

They need my superior brain to free them from this pooch prison.

ZzZz^zz z z

Sweet dreams for now, you horrible hound.
Soon you'll **sleep out in the doghouse for good!**

MONTY DREAMS ABOUT...

... frolicking with bunnies.

... romantic dinners for two.

... boxing the furry feline, Mr. Famous.

COCO DREAMS ABOUT . . .

. . . buying Monty a first-class ticket to Nowhere.

. . . locking Monty out of the house.

. . . sending Monty to doggy jail.

Naptime is over, you ninny. It is time to show the humans what a mess you've made.

That's right, you oaf. Chase me around. Wreck the house. You are behaving beautifully . . .

if you want to be banished, that is!

Five minutes from now, the house will be trashed, Coach will be steamed, and Monty—**that miserable mongrel—will be out on his rump.**

PARKER?
WHAT'S THAT RACKET?
IF THAT DOG IS CAUSING TROUBLE,

HE BETTER
PACK HIS
BAGS.

Arf!

Chapter 7

RULE #5

IF YOUR NAME IS NOT "TRASH," STAY OUT OF THE CAN

Loyal reader, isn't this all so thrilling?

While **Parker** tries to convince the hairy one that **everything is fine,** Monty the ragamuffin is **destroying** the house!

Why do dogs devour garbage? Is the flavor of moldy potatoes and rotten tomatoes irresistable? Why can't canines resist a can of crud? Are they drawn to the delicate scent of sour milk and used tissues?

Surely science must provide an explanation.

The truth is . . .

I DON'T CARE!

All that matters is that this stinking mound of scum is Monty's one-way ticket to Nowhere Land.*

* I hope he sends me a postcard once he gets there!
  I need some new cage lining.

How will he leave his messy mark?

Let me count the ways . . .

#1 Coffeepot polluted

#2 Drawers defiled

#3 Saucepan spilled

#4 Dog food destroyed

Parker will **never** right this wreckage before Coach sees it. And that means **bon voyage, Bozo!**

#7 Flowers flopped

#6 Trash tipped

#5 Oven opened

#8 Stool slayed

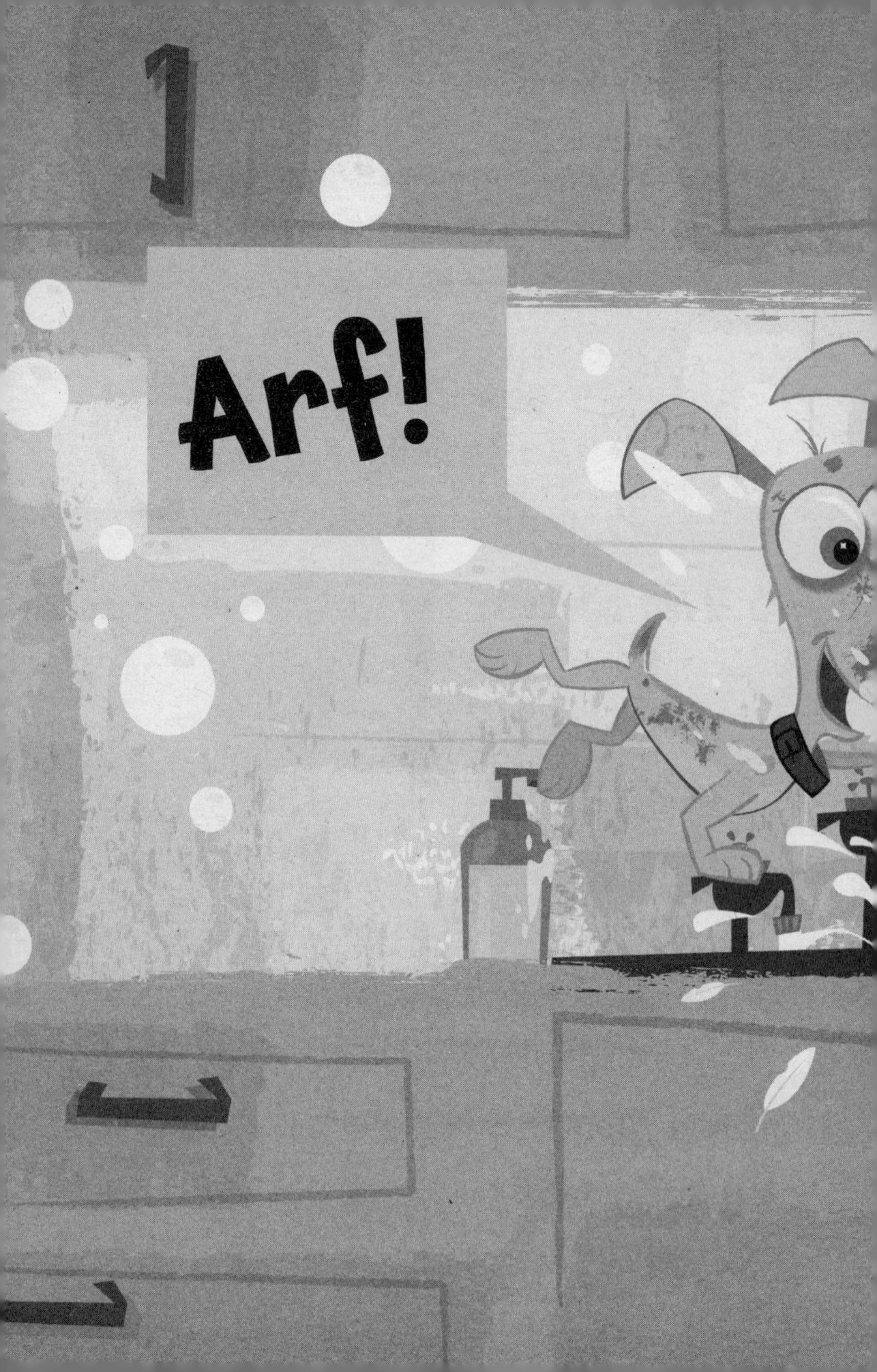
Arf!

Monty, stay **focused** on making a mess. This is no time for a **sudsy slide on the kitchen floor,** Sir **Smellsalot.**

PARKER!

IS THAT THE TRASH-CAN LID
I HEAR SWINGING?

**DID I HEAR THE DOG
BOWL SKID?**

IF I SEE SO MUCH AS A CRUMB
ON THE KITCHEN FLOOR . . .

The time for banishment has finally come! Happy day! The small human will never be able to explain that mongrel's mess.

How has Monty laundered his litter? Let me count the ways . . .

#1 Coffeepot cleaned

#2 Drawers defended

#3 Saucepan sponged

#4 Dog food doctored

#6 Trash tidied

#7 Flowers fixed

#5 Oven occupied

#8 Stool stabilized

What?

How?

Impossible!

Smile away, scalawag.

Enjoy this minor glory for now.

I'll wipe that **dopey grin** off your face.

I've got one final trick up my sleeve. . . .

Chapter 8

RULE #7

MR. FAMOUS IS NOT A TOY

Skillful reader, feast your eyes on **this**. The hopeful human has let **Death Breath** go outside and escape the scene of his latest crime.

But Parker has forgotten the temptations of the backyard. Monty cannot help **digging unsightly holes** or **howling at earsplitting volumes**.

But these are small problems compared to the big rule the beast is about to break. . . .

The dirty dingbat is looking high and low for the feline he only *thinks* is his friend.

Enter Mr. Famous, the neighbors' snobby cat.

NAME:

Mr. Famous

FAVORITE FOOD: *caviar, Kobe beef, and truffles*

FUR COLOR: *auburn with blonde and russet highlights*

PET PEEVE: *signing autographs*

SIZE: *small and dainty*

HOW MR. FAMOUS GOT...
FAMOUS

Born with naturally silky fur, long whiskers, and an expressive tail.

Received a star on the Hollywood Walk of Fame!

Snagged a Hollywood agent.

Promoted cat food in a Super Bowl commercial.

Gave a moving performance in a summer blockbuster.

Clearly, Mr. Famous is out of Monty's league.

When the **furry fleabag** suggests a game of Chase-Your-Tail-Like-a-Buffoon with our neighborhood celebrity, the two creatures do not see snout to snout.

Monty wants to play, but Mr. Famous only
wants to primp and preen.

But does Monty take the hint? Nope,
not even when Mr. Famous
ignores his tricks . . .

. . . **overlooks** his dance moves . . .

... and **tunes out** his predictions.

But what's this? The Flaming Pins of Fear seem to be getting a reaction from our little celebrity.

Unfortunately, hiding in the treetops is not the reaction Monty was hoping for.

Ha-ha! The neighbors will be furious that Mutt Mouth has scared their talented tabby up a tree. **Oh, happy day!** The sun is shining and the bees are buzzing in celebration of Monty's impending banishment.

BUZZzZZz z

WHY BEES ARE A BIRD'S BEST FRIEND

Bees can fly, and never stink up the house. Best yet, they seem to like Monty about as much as I do. See them work their itchy-twitchy magic on the four-legged blockhead. Monty, watch out for their stingers!

Gleeful glory! The sting of my winged sister has made Monty lose his mind! **Up like a rocket he goes!** I see a one-way ticket to Outer Dogsville in his future. Time to alert the hairy human!

SQUAWK!

But what's this? Mr. Famous hitching a ride on the flying fleabag? Monty saving the cat?

It can't be true!

Oh, misfortune! Coach has arrived at just the wrong moment. Instead of a **ruckus** he sees a **rescue**!

Chapter 9

EVERY DOG HAS HIS DAY

Unfair world! It's clear that Monty is no good. He should have been banished long ago.

Deported for devouring the meat loaf!

Sent away for spoiling the sofa!

Evicted for eating shorts!

Transported for terrifying the cat!

But somehow that miserable mutt always wiggles his way to forgiveness and reward!

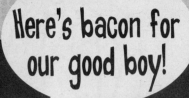

121

Monty is crude!

He's rude!

I am **superior!**

Monty is inferior!

He's vile!

He's a monster!

He must be
DEFEATED!!!

RACKET? WE HAVE GOT TO GET THIS BIRD TO BEHAVE! ...ERY TIME I TURN A... ...S SQUAWKING ...ABOU... ...OR SCREECHING ...OUT THAT... I SHOULD BE ABLE ... GET SOM... PEACE AND QUIET ...N MY OWN ...ME. I JUST WANT ... E ABLE TO ...OY MY STINKING MEA... ...OAF WITHOUT ...S FEATHER FACE CH...PING AWAY LI... LUNATIC! I'M AT...

GASP! The hairy one! He just said,
"Banishment."

But his finger! Is pointing!

At ME?!?

124

Me? Banished? How could this be? What could I have done to deserve such a ghastly fate?

Sweet reader, Monty is free to rule the house, and I—the Lane family's loyal friend and companion—am exiled in disgrace. The tables have turned. Oh, sorry day!

PARKER'S TOOLS FOR TEACHING AN OLD DOG NEW TRICKS

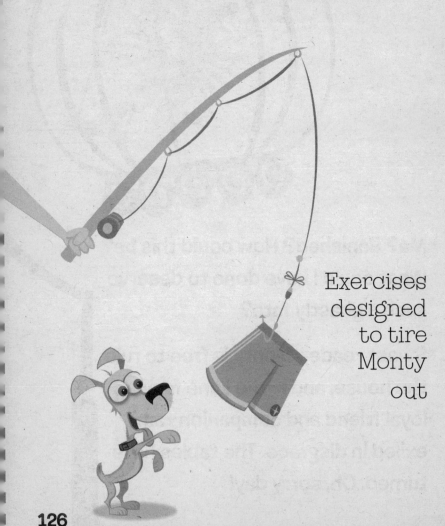

Exercises designed to tire Monty out

Meat-loaf flavored dog food

A cozy home away from home for Monty when the family needs a break

Banishment
Bed & Breakfast

THE END!*

* No, it's not! Someday I will return and give that mangy mongrel exactly what he deserves! I will prevail! You'll see. . . .